Adam & Eve's
Ashes

Magnetic Pole Shift,
Ancient Prophecy & Catastrophism

C. Elmon Meade

Dedication

This book is dedicated to the memory of my favorite Editor-in-Chief and my Mamaw, Margaret Pauline (Meade) Worley. Her frail body failed on July 1st of 2023, but her Soul soared through the Heavens to be with Jesus Christ our Lord and Savior. Her spirit, character, and love for her family lives on to this day. May she praise the King of kings without ceasing until we can join her in Glory! Thank you, Jesus!

Table of Contents

Acknowledgments

I would first like to acknowledge the Hopi Nation and all of my Native American/ Indigenous brothers and sisters. Regardless of your tribal affiliation or blood quantum, know that I see you. I feel the presence of our ancestors and I respect our Red Nation in everything I strive to do. Perhaps Chief Crazy Horse said it best when he said: "The Red Nation shall rise again and it shall be a blessing for a sick world; a world filled with broken promises, selfishness, and separations; a world longing for light again." Mitakuye Oyasin.

A special shout-out to my phenomenal care team at the Norman Fixel Institute For Neurological Diseases (UF - Gainesville). I have been under their care for all of 2023 for Deep Brain Stimulation to treat my Young-Onset Parkinson's disease. This all-star collection of Movement Disorder rock stars includes my neurosurgeon Dr. Justin "The Artifact" Hilliard, Dr. Bhavana Patel, Dr. Christopher Hess, Kendra D. Murphy, PA-C, Abigail Corriveau, APRN, and the godfather himself, Dr. Michael Okun.

Also, I must give credit to the pioneers of Catastrophism. Without their knowledge, persistence, and tough skin, my story would not be possible. This list of titans includes Jean-André DeLuc, Georges Cuvier, Dr. Immanuel Velikovsky, J. Harlen Bretz, Charles Hapgood, Albert Einstein, Dr. Chauncey "Chan" Powers Thomas, Maj. Maynard E. White, Adm. Richard E. Byrd, Dr. Anthony L. Peratt, Dr. Robert Shoch, Dr. J.E.T. Channel (also from UF), Douglas Vogt, David Talbot, Andrew Hall, Randall Carlson, Michael Steinbacher, Dr. August Dunning, and last, but certainly not least Ben Davidson.

Finally, I want to thank my family, my church family, and my Lord and Savior Jesus Christ. He has set before us the most perfect example of living a humble, passionate, and extraordinary life. Seek Him and find serenity, hope, and everlasting life. Aho and Amen.

Chapter 1

My Introduction to Catastrophism

"...at each point on the Earth's surface that has been carefully studied, many climatic changes have taken place, apparently quite suddenly.

...[crustal] displacements may take place as the consequence of comparatively slight forces exerted on the crust, derived from the Earth's momentum of rotation, which in turn will tend to alter the axis of rotation of the Earth's crust."

– Albert Einstein

I n the winter of 2023, I happened upon a YouTube video titled "CIA Classified Book about the Pole Shift, Mass Extinctions and The True Adam & Eve Story." While the title is long, the video was definitely not short on terrifying scenarios and imagery about the end of the modern world. This video was a review of a declassified book entitled "The Adam and Eve Story" by McDonnell Douglas engineer Dr. Chan Thomas. The story is about a 90-degrees magnetic pole shift which flips the earth on its side within a day. (Check out the video on the YouTube channel *The Why Files.*)

The video got my curiosity fired up, and I researched anything and everything I could about the likelihood of the Chan Thomas story. Much to my surprise, I discovered that a majority of the scenarios laid out by Dr. Thomas were legit! A man named Dr. Charles Hapgood wrote a book in 1958 titled "The Path of the Pole." In this work, he explained his Earth Crust Displacement Theory. He even received tacit approval for his theory by having none other than renowned physicist Albert Einstein write the foreword for his book. One problem: although Einstein worked out the math of Hapgood's theory, he still could not figure out the event or set of circumstances around what would kick-start such a calamity. Enter space weather expert and researcher Ben Davidson of Suspicious Observers.

Ben Davidson has been at the forefront of sounding the alarms about a phenomenon called the solar micro nova. Most of us have heard of the death of a star as the star *going supernova* or even *Hypernova*. However, recent discoveries have vindicated Ben's work by proving that some stars keep banging over time (repeatedly) instead of doing it just once and then dying. Welcome to the utterly horrifying event known as a solar micro nova!

A solar micro nova is an energetic expulsion of the outside shell of a star. Think of a large X-class solar flare or Coronal Mass Ejection (CME); only happening across the entire surface of our star. This eruption is caused in one of two ways: 1) material accretion and/or 2) a magnetic kick. Scary enough, our galactic current sheet provides both ingredients! The galactic current sheet contains massive amounts of dust, Energetic Neutral Atoms (ENAs), and electrically charged ions at a higher density than the ambient interstellar space, as well as containing the magnetic reversal point of the galaxy. That is both a magnetic kick and material being dumped onto our star to induce a micro nova event. Just know that if, no, make that when our sun goes micro nova, we will have mere minutes to save satellites, power down grids, and to seek immediate shelter if you are on the side of the globe facing the sun. Within hours, all hell will break loose!

This is where my updated retelling of Dr. Chan Thomas' epic tale named for Adam and Eve comes in. The micro nova has happened. What now? My updated take of "The Adam and Eve Story" corrects some inaccuracies made in Dr. Thomas' original version. For instance, the wind will still attack us, just not at 1,000 MPH, as previously believed. I have corrected the wind speeds and direction — the seas will push northward instead of from west to east, then slosh back towards the south. Regardless, this version of the next catastrophe will still bottleneck the gene pool of humanity; just as it did following the Toba supervolcano eruption, the "Great Flood" of Gilgamesh, Noah, and others, and the Gothenburg Magnetic Excursion, which closely aligns with the Younger Dryas event. This is not a feel-good story, where it's man vs. nature and man has the just-in-time victory over the end of the world, as in a Hollywood movie. You can't have Catastrophism without catastrophes. However, I appreciate Ben Davidson's mantra and sign-off of "Eyes Open, No Fear." Fear is a paralyzer and now is not the time for paralysis. Always seek resiliency by being strong in mind, body, and spirit. I will leave you with my personal mantra: pray, prep, and keep watch, my friends.

> "Therefore **keep watch**, because you do not know the day or the hour."
>
> — Matthew 25:13 NIV

> "Behold, I come as a thief. Blessed is he that **watcheth**..."
>
> — Revelation 16:15 KJV

Chapter 2

Chan Thomas Redux: Catastrophism Reimagined

An imperceptible force awakens beneath the earth's crust. Coaxed into motion by an electromagnetic assault from our sun. The plasma helio-weapon of choice is a series of deadly Coronal Mass Ejections (CME) of the likes that this current generation has not witnessed. Remnants of a massive blue comet, a sungrazer named Comet Woods-Monard 73, attacked our star after exploding into dozens of cosmic missiles much like Comet Shoemaker-Levy 9 four decades earlier. The resulting dust and debris from the dying comet, along with a wave of dust and particulates from the galactic current sheet, has caused a series of life-threatening CMEs followed by a micro nova of our star. The accretion of galactic dust and leftover particulate from the comet have set off an irreversible chain of global extinction-level events.

The resulting micro nova has the outer shell of the sun, densely packed with plasma energy and star metals, exploding out in all directions, and now speeding towards the earth. This solar attack unlocks the earth's crust at the low velocity zone by canceling the thermoelectric equilibrium that keeps the entire crust in place. The weight of the ice on Greenland, and to a lesser extent, the Arctic winter's sea ice, has begun its migration towards a new equatorial home. Eventually, Greenland, Alaska, and Antarctica will straddle the equator.

The low rumble, noticed only by pets and wildlife at first, then by seismometers everywhere, is just a prelude to the global catastrophe building beneath everyone's feet. The global *kill shot* has done more than just knock out power grids across the entire globe months earlier. It has also energized the molten shell between the earth's crust and the uppermost layer of the mantle. Yes, enduring the loss of electricity and end of the digital age less than a year earlier is tough, but the red skies over Europe, Africa, and the Atlantic Ocean predict a penultimate doom. Is this the red horse, the second of the Four Horsemen from the Book of Revelation? Wars and rumors of war have preceded this cataclysm going back to Cain killing Abel. However, this episode of global bloodshed has just begun.

Now the "earth turns over" just as Immanuel Velikovsky predicted. A horrific 90-degrees tilt of the earth in which the weight of ice packs in Greenland and Antarctica precipitates the 12,000-year cyclical catastrophe foretold by so many from humanity's past. Once dismissed as legends told by seers, shamans, or modern-day pseudo-scientists, the bill has come due, and humanity will struggle to survive. T. S. Eliot stands avenged; the world as we know it goes out with a whimper.

The red sky seen around half of the world takes on a different countenance in central Africa in the moments prior to the 90-degree rotation of the earth. Countries north of the Okavango Delta now understand the ancients who built Machu Picchu who foretold a day without sunset as the earth jerks to a standstill before a third of the stars fell from their sky. Where did they land, you ask? They did not land on earth but fell out of view as the earth rolled forward out of their cosmic flight pattern. A red sun, although still burning white hot, now appears black and locks into place over the ancestral homeland of homo sapiens. A similar mechanism, albeit from a magnetic excursion and not a micro nova, caused northern Africa's once lush green pastures and woodlands to become a barren wasteland over 6,000 years ago. Fast forward to a new Sahara desert emerging to the south; laid waste by the plasma bombardment from the dusty black heart of the sun. Squatter man dances in place, then tilts over, dragging Iberia towards the equator. The squatter man tilts, the turning over of the earth, a tipping of the scales carried by he who rode the black horse: our worst nightmares are being revealed. The black sun stalks its prey for the next three days and this stellar hunter is ravenous!

The expansive grasslands and rainforest biomes of central Africa die an instantaneous death. Flash fried not by an overabundance of carbon, but by a solar micro nova brought on by the prophesied Hopi blue star of death — albeit a comet in this lifetime. The South Atlantic Anomaly, an area of lower geomagnetic strength, further exacerbates the solar forcing at the lower levels of the remaining atmosphere over central Africa and South America. In some spots of this anomaly, earth's magnetic shield is down to only 25% of its original strength. Now the red sun has given way to an all-consuming fire lit by Ra; all at once and everywhere. Simultaneous ignition of the magma underfoot and buried under oceans now bursting forth in fiery jets of explosive steam and liquid fire. Everything and everyone burns from the *earth fire*, bursting forth from miles within the earth. Say goodbye to the Hopi fourth world; will there be a fifth?

Soon, the sun shines no more in the smoke and ash-filled sky. This must have been what the inhabitants of Pompei had experienced long ago. Most of the continent that gave birth to the mighty Egyptians, if not the entire human race, joins Atlantis, Lemuria, and Mu at the bottom of the watery abyss. Even the mighty sphinx cannot withstand this firestorm soon followed by a slosh back flood from the Mediterranean Sea. Mankind thought the mountains of broiling hot Saharan sand were impenetrable for centuries, but soon those same sand dunes will transform to a soupy confluence of saltwater and mud. These slosh back floods will repeat on every landmass and will be far more destructive than the initial inundation.

From destruction also comes creation, and this is the case all along the Great Rift region of southeastern Africa and the Levant. The excitement and activation of the Large Low-Shear Velocity Province (LLSVP) deep within the earth's mantle provides a measure of hope to future generations in parts of Africa. The earth's crust breaks loose in enormous plates and begins an upwelling process which would save some from the impending floods. Eastern Africa will have a net gain of landmass from the cataclysm, but for whom? Survivors are few. Will the newborns of the fifth world remember the pyramids now buried under miles of mud and the weight of the Mediterranean?

As if this hurricane of fire and smoke is not enough to signal the apocalypse, now the earth's oceans will have their say. The icy waters of the South Atlantic pile up and seem to hesitate before unleashing an insurmountable amount of kinetic energy on the scorched coastlines from Montevideo to the Caribbean. A wall of water half a mile in height moves across the scorched beaches and continues to rise with the land, as if pushed by an unknown force. The invisible force is winds over 250 MPH sustained and gusting to nearly 400 MPH. Winds usually reserved for Jupiter's *Great Red Spot* and *Little Red Spot* lift everything into the disturbed atmosphere and pull trees, structures, and man northward. A relentless blitzkrieg from the earth's winds — the destruction is unceasing and complete. Those who do not die from the shockwave will do so from many injuries sustained from being slammed into buildings or punctured by insurmountable amounts of airborne debris. Should one survive the initial gauntlet, they will then be greeted with water hazards like downed trees, light poles, and vehicles of all types. The winds and the waters are full of hazards.

Monstrous waves devastate not only because of their speed and height but also from the overwhelming weight they carry. The Brazilian coast is no match for the sheer volume of unending flood waters displacing sand, soil, and rock. High-rises all along the picturesque beaches of South America topple like dominos, kicked over by Neptune himself. Soon, the southern Gulf of Mexico fills with hundreds, if not thousands, of feet of mud, debris, and the dead. The snowcapped Andes look on in mournful reverence, knowing their home continent will never be the same.

Meanwhile, in the United States, curious onlookers fill every beach in Florida, peering upward at the red sun and pinkish auroras and clouds. Without warning, curiosity turns to stunned silence as the once tranquil waterfront retreats to the horizon. Tectonic plates slamming and sinking an ocean away now show their continent killing force as an epic tsunami. The low, distant rumble heard by all is now replaced with an eerie silence, but not for long. The Atlantic Ocean begins the attack while the Gulf of Mexico, also energized by volcanic and tectonic energy, provides the second of a destructive one-two punch. Tallahassee, named from the Muskogean word for *Old Town*, now sinks beneath the waves and mud of a *new sea*. The screams and cries of the dying now fill the air. Is this the macabre music of Atlantis?

The mighty Mississippi river now serves as a conduit of death and destruction as it funnels rising waters inland. The middle of the continent from Texas to the Great Lakes will soon join Florida in its watery grave. Mount Mitchell and Grandfather Mountain in North Carolina stand tall as two witnesses of God's wrath, like Elijah and Moses. Handfuls of survivors either cling to treetops while others float away in boats or makeshift rafts. The once violent waves now wrap around the tallest of mountaintops, filling every single valley below.

As waters continue to rise across the American heartland, an additional threat emerges out west. This is not a run-of-the-mill earthquake like the ones Californians have grown used to or, yes, even complacent to during their lifetimes. A global earthquake is steadily building into a penultimate crescendo of destruction and cataclysm that will reset the entire face of our world. Nearly every dormant caldera and volcano across the globe ignites with a slow, effusive outflow. A new reality explodes forth in the Pacific Northwest, Alaska, and other spots across the vast Pacific Ocean. In fact, the Hawaiian Islands vault skyward, as if birthing a capital for a new continental landmass. Is this the birthing pangs of a new Lemuria? This brings little solace to the citizens of Hawaii as high-rise hotels, homes, and roadways shake violently until they crumble to dust.

As the earth begins to move and sway all along the Pacific *Ring of Fire*, the California mountains no longer stand in silence, but bow at the feet of an unseen master. Rolling, tumbling, and racing towards the sea. A groan intimating an off-key trumpet emits from the heart of Mt. Shasta and the many ridgelines to the north reveal their deadly secret, exploding into enormous plumes of ash, pyroclastic flows, and jets of liquid fire borne from the earth's bowels.

Hood, Mount St. Helens, and Rainier erupt with fury and anger to proclaim to the world they are dormant no more! Pyroclastic flows level forests, scorches valleys, and kills man and beast alike. The 1980 eruption of Mount St. Helens does not come close to the death toll of these combined volcanic disasters. While flood waters and tidal waves inundate most of the continental United States, the Pacific Northwest erupts into a roaring inferno. If only the continental floods could put out these volcanic fires, but alas. The standing order of the day for the northwest is for the earth fire to rage and burn!

The Ring of Fire is far from finished with the disastrous upheaval afflicting the lower forty-eight. Volcanoes in the Aleutian Islands of Alaska join in on the destructive orgy. The rest of Alaska's volcanoes follow suit and the Alaskan Oil Pipeline lights up like a roman candle. Alaskan taiga and permafrost get a head start on their meltdown that would have happened anyway once Alaska moves to its new home atop earth's equator. American survivors are few and cling to life almost wholly in the Rockies and North Carolina mountains. Will they someday join up with survivors from Europe and Asia to rebuild the world they once knew?

On the other side of North America, Greenland has trekked southward to the torrid zone. The equatorial, tropical heat causes instant melting of the ice atop Greenland. Enormous amounts of solid ice now transition into a gaseous state via super-evaporation. Water vapor saturates the atmosphere all along the middle of the globe. Water, which was once locked away in ice, but no longer thanks to equatorial, tropical heat, shrouds earth's atmosphere in a gray, hyper evaporation-induced fog.

Cosmic Ray forcing into the L-shell of the ionosphere carved an enormous scar into the middle of Greenland prior to its journey south. What appears to be a miniature, charred version of the Grand Canyon now scars the subcontinent from Nord in the north to Nuuk in the south. American elected officials, Pentagon brass, and a select few huddle in tunnels beneath

Thule Air Force Base, not knowing what the days ahead will bring. Is there a country left to govern?

Europe fares no better than the Americas. Europe is all but obliterated by a gargantuan wave of water and mud pushed by an unrelenting wind. The Carpathian Mountains, once home to Vlad the Impaler, do not stand a chance against the roiling tempest churning across the whole of Europe. The Pyrenees Mountains tumble to meet the new inland sea within hours. Only the highest of peaks within the French and Swiss Alps and the Caucuses survive to tell the tale of the end of man. Rocks and boulders of the Scandinavian Mountains cry out in silence before most of the peaks settle into their new underwater home. However, the Svalbard Global Seed Vault is somehow saved from the danger imposed by the rising tide. One glimmer of hope for a waterlogged Europe and a gob smacked human race.

Big Ben, Buckingham Palace, and Stonehenge are only memories now. The uncaring winds from the south shredded modern-day tourist attractions all across London. One might think the stone monoliths of Stonehenge were safe from the tornadic winds; however, even the blue-stones of mighty Stonehenge succumb to violent slosh back floods. Great Britain joins ancient Doggerland and mythical Hy-Brasil in an unimaginable homecoming under the turbulent surf.

Iceland was first submerged beneath the initial onslaught of the perturbed Atlantic. However, as the highest waves roll forward to attack the Norwegian coast, the land of fire and ice roars back to life with the awakening of Vulcan, Hephaestus, and Surtur; a grand meeting of volcano gods bursting above the water to form new land. This Phoenix-like rebirth from fire is little consolation to the dead. The inhabitants of Reykjavik, much like London, Paris, Berlin and so many others lie in ruins. Lifeless. Still. Only salty tears within an unending ocean of despair.

The Vatican suffers additional insult thanks to the Campi Flegrei volcano eruption to its south. While the long feared supervolcano eruption did not take place, tons of sulfur dioxide were released from its effusive eruption. These volcanic compounds turned into sulfuric acid once suspended within the Italian cloud cover. Man and beast died of asphyxiation, while the volcanic compounds scarred or disfigured monuments and structures forever. The poisonous cloud afforded very few enough time for last rites before succumbing to the encroaching Mediterranean.

In a land that used to be at the bottom of the world, the Taupō Volcano on New Zealand's north island erupts forth in a hyper-eruption. This super-volcano, unlike Yellowstone and others, did not hold back! Ejecta from deep within the earth's crust blasts forth like foam from a firehose, bouncing off of the earth's atmosphere. The supervolcano ejects fiery magma and rocks, varying in size from gravel to small mountains to bombard the southern hemisphere. The cities of eastern Australia and the villages of Papua New Guinea reel from the unceasing brimstone bombardment.

Taupō's eruption obliterates Auckland and Sydney while New Caledonia and Vanuatu have their own volcanic eruptions to endure. Within mere days, the sea floor will rise, and a new theorized Zealandia will be born from the chaos. As most of Australia sinks beneath the waves, Zealandia rises to greet the new purified world; in all of her smokey, noxious haze.

The slosh back floods shred the rest of the island nations of Asia, Japan, the Philippines, and Indonesia to pieces. What few survivors once clung to life in the mountains are now once and for all swept away to watery graves. The actions of a single madman destroyed North and South Korea in a nuclear nightmare, only months earlier, and they cannot muster the strength to mourn this newest calamity. The radioactive ashes welcome the cool waters.

Survivors in the Caucasus, Urals, and Central Asian Steppe realize they are ill-prepared to live and thrive in this new upside-down world. Most will freeze to death long before spending a complete 24 hours at the top of the frozen globe. The southernmost waters of the Bay of Bengal off the coast of India now mark the new North Pole. Meanwhile, the new South Pole rests somewhere off the western coast of South America. One may imagine the spirits of ancient Tiwanaku and Machu Picchu wrestling for control over the pole. Many of the initial survivors on the Indian subcontinent and in the warm, tropical regions of Brazil were flash frozen in less than an hour of the earth turning over. Extreme temperature change coupled with cosmic ray forcing was too much for mammalian life to withstand.

On the seventh day, the floodwaters recede, and the molten fury of earth fire seems to subside. Small, ragtag groups of survivors, spread across the four corners of the globe, attempt to pick up the pieces of the world they once knew, and take stock of what little remains. They will scratch and claw their way to a new primary goal — survival. Life almost always persists, and this time should be no different. Life will carry on now as well, even if the world has fallen over and nothing will ever be the same again.

The solar micro nova has abruptly plunged humanity back to the Stone Age. Perhaps humanity will come back to its collective senses, reject the modernity that once turned hearts cold and flesh evil, and turn back to the ways of our ancestors. Back to a lasting peace for all nations. A brotherhood of mankind. Connectedness, kindness, and a Godly love that overcomes all and will endure forever.

> *"Let all bitterness, and wrath, and anger, and clamour, and evil speaking, be put away from you, with all malice: And be ye kind to one another, tenderhearted, forgiving one another, even as God for Christ's sake hath forgiven you."*
>
> *– Ephesians 4:31-32 (KJV)*

> *"But the fruit of the Spirit is love, joy, peace, longsuffering, gentleness, goodness, faith, Meekness, temperance: against such there is no law."*
>
> *– Galatians 5:-23 (KJV)*

Chapter 3

Signs and Cosmic Warnings

T his section will offer the reader a list of organized signs to be on the lookout for regarding magnetic pole shift, a solar super-flare/ CME event, and/or a micro nova of our sun. Some items on this list will require additional research, some are my own prognostications, and others are already well under way and being observed around the globe. This comprehensive list is dynamic and will undoubtedly change over time as will our climate, planet, solar system, and universe. Change is inevitable, but being unaware and unprepared is not. Prioritize the things you and your family can control, plan accordingly to your specific circumstances, and keep watch.

Weather & Climate

- Weather events once thought of as rare begin happening with increasing frequency: blizzards in Death Valley, springtime snow/ice in TX/AZ, deadly heat waves in Siberia in the middle of winter, etc. (wild temperature swings daily)

- Mega-droughts, mega-floods, and ARkStorms: rainfall totals will begin breaking all known records (yearly, monthly, daily, hourly)

- Increase in number and severity of prolonged derecho storms

- Unusual cyclonic activity: hurricanes in the Mediterranean Sea, Ireland, Spain and cyclones in southern Australia, South Africa, etc.

- Persistent Dansgaard-Oeschger (DO) Event moves from localized cooling to a global event

- Release of the Beaufort Gyre and reduced salinity in the North Atlantic
- Slowdown of ocean currents and/or shutdown of the Atlantic Meridional Overturning Circulation (AMOC)/ Gulf Stream
- Increased extreme lightning storms, lightning from the ground, & "balls" of lightning seen worldwide
- Sharp increase in the number of named storms (tropical and subtropical) in the same basin at the same time (i.e.: seven named storms in the Atlantic Ocean at once)

"After this, I saw four angels standing at the four corners of the earth, holding back the four winds of the earth, so that no wind would blow on the earth or on the sea or on any tree."

– Revelation 7:1

Geological Changes

- Increased seismic activity at super volcanoes in Campi Flegrei, Italy or Taupō, New Zealand
- Earth spins faster (shortest day records set weekly/ daily)
- Increased earthquake activity
- Increase in ambient static electricity at all elevations
- Increase in frequency of low latitude pink and red auroras
- USGS and NOAA ocean buoys detect sea floor rise and/or warming of seafloor vents

"But the day that Lot went out of Sodom it rained fire and brimstone from Heaven, and destroyed them all."

– Luke 17:29

Solar Electromagnetic Assault Imminent!

- Sharp increase in sunspot activity, size, and development
- Solar maximum arrives increasingly earlier with each cycle (11-year cycle becomes 10- or 9-year return to maximum)
- Weakening of earth's magnetosphere results in greater impacts from M-class solar flares
- Multiple X-class solar flares aimed at earth
- Power plant fires, transformers exploding at low latitudes, tv and radio waves interruption/ failure, copper wiring melting, and electrical/ fiber optic cable failures
- Near global GPS failures
- Loss of contact with satellites and/or complete failure (go offline, then fall back to earth)
- Grounding of all air travel and/or planes drop out of the sky
- Collapse of electric grids (global grid failure possible)

"And it shall come to pass in that day, saith the Lord God, that I will cause the sun to go down at noon, and I will darken the earth in the clear day:"

– Amos 8:9

"Let the stars of the twilight thereof be dark; let it look for light, but have none; neither let it see the dawning of the day:"

– Job 3:9

Solar System Changes

- Dust arrives first at the Oort Cloud and continues to accumulate, moving inward towards the Sun

- Increased seismic activity detected on the moons of Uranus, Saturn, Jupiter, and on the surface of Pluto, Ceres, Triton, and Mars

- Increase in seismic microquake swarms at the north pole of Mars

- Increase in clouds, wind speed, and storms observed on Neptune, Uranus, Saturn, and Jupiter

- Off-season, self-contained, and persistent sandstorms on Mars

- Emergence of counter-rotating vortices at the poles of Venus coupled with temperature and barometric pressure rise

> *"And there will be signs in the sun, in the moon, and in the stars; and on the earth distress of nations, with perplexity, the sea and the waves roaring."*
>
> *– Luke 21:25*

Brain and Heart Health

- Increase in cardiac events and deaths from heart attacks (all ages and backgrounds)

- Unexplained spike in hardware failure of pacemaker and other electrical medical device implants

- Irregular animal and human behavior because of impacts on the hippocampus and locus coeruleus regions of the brain (fear, anxiety, aggressiveness, fight or flight, panic, judgment impairment, psychosis, widespread mental exhaustion and/ or breakdowns)

- Global reports of disturbed migration patterns and timing of migrations (out of sync)

- Animals seen exhibiting confusion, unexplained aggression, refusing to eat/ drink, and "self-herding" in circular and octagonal patterns

- Sharp increase in road rage and willful disobedience to societal rules and laws

- Increased crime (property & violent crime), widespread dissociative behaviors, and/or rise in antisocial & sociopathy tendencies

"Men's hearts failing them from fear and the expectation of those things which are coming on the earth, for the powers of the heavens will be shaken."

– Luke 21:26

"The end of everything is near. Therefore, practice self-control, and keep your minds clear so that you can pray. Above all, love each other warmly, because love covers many sins."

– 1 Peter 4:7-8

Popular Culture Shifts

- Cultural shift away from traditions (holidays, traditional family units), institutions (mass media, courts, elections, post-secondary education), and religion/ spirituality (churches, ceremonies, covenants, marriage)

- Curb population growth through effeminizing and/or a-sexualizing the male population through overt means (pop culture reinforcement, corporate intrusions into private life, negative impacts to social credit score for perceived "toxic masculinity") and covert means (chemical toxicity, food supply restrictions, promotion of prescription drugs in place of natural foods)

- Curb population growth (Part 2): proliferation of "on-demand" abortion, medical-assisted suicide without limits, and capital punishment for political prisoners

- Legalization and mainstream proliferation of psychotropic drugs
- End goal of criminalizing so-called "toxic masculinity" is to prevent armed insurrections, civil wars and other extra-political activities which would undermine globalist Elites

"Take heart, I have overcome the world."

– John 16:33

"Above all else, guard your heart, for everything you do flows from it."

– Proverbs 4:23

Government Actions/ Inaction

Uncontrollable & reckless spending by world governments

- Rise in and concerted effort to spread misinformation and disinformation; especially in "The West" (i.e.: carbon/ CO_2 vs. solar electromagnetism)
- Governmental transparency is sacrificed for the benefit of the Elites and politically connected (governments obfuscate pole shift/ solar micro nova threat and hide blackout plans which intentionally omit the masses)
- World governments will attempt to control their respective populations by restricting freedoms of press, speech, movement, self-determination, religion, and due process
- World governments will abdicate responsibilities of governance and self-defense to world agencies and world bodies (UN, EU, NATO, IPCC, WHO, et al.)

"Be always on the watch, and pray that you may be able to escape all that is about to happen, and that you may be able to stand before the Son of Man."

– Luke 21:36

Chapter 4

The Hopi Tablets

"...the first world was destroyed by an all-consuming fire that came from above and from below. The second world was shaken until it shifted from its axis, and everything froze in ice. The third world ended with a global flood. The current world is the fourth and its destiny is in our hands. The Creator watches and is prepared to grab it with two hands!"

– Hopi Nation Prophecy

I took the following notes from Dr. Lee Brown's (Cherokee) speech at the 1986 Continental Indigenous Council in Fairbanks, Alaska. The preceding paragraphs will retell and paraphrase Mr. Brown's presentment of the Hopi prophetic story. In 1992, Hopi Elder Thomas Banyacya spoke about the Hopi Prophecy at the United Nations General Assembly Hall. Both men spoke about the Hopi tablets and Prophecy Rock in their own way, with respect and reverence as true Wisdom Keepers. *My commentary will be in italics to differentiate my own original thoughts from those of Dr. Brown's speech.*

Prophecy Rock is on the Hopi Reservation, Arizona, and from the Native worldview, we (fellow Native Americans) consider the Hopi and all Native peoples to be part of the Red people of the East. It is said more tablets are in Switzerland (North/White), Mount Kenya (West/Black), and Tibet (South/Yellow), which sits on the opposite side of the globe from Hopi lands. Is it coincidence alone that the Hopi word for sun is *taawa,* whereas the Tibetan word for moon (the inverse of the sun) is *dawa? Or is coincidence itself merely another way for Unetlanvhi (Our Creator) to show us potential knowledge and understanding, one small piece at a time?*

In the beginning, there was a cycle of the Spirit. Then, the cycle of the mineral (rock) preceded the cycle of the plant. Now we are in the cycle of the animals. As we come to the end of that cycle, we begin the cycle of the human being. Once we are immersed into the cycle of the human being, the highest and greatest powers that we have will be released to us. These powers include biology, chemistry, geology, mathematics, and many, many other forms of scientific knowledge. Modern-day wonders like unlocking the mysteries of Deoxyribose Nucleic Acid (DNA), gene splicing, cloning, space travel, and nuclear energy are part of this transference of scientific knowhow from the Great Spirit, who created everything seen and unseen.

From time to time, the Great Spirit comes down to earth via a Great Messenger to warn the people. The Great Spirit came down without a messenger at the beginning of time and gathered the earth's people onto an island which has since disappeared beneath the sea. The Great Spirit told them, "I am going to send you out into the four directions to the four corners of the world, and over time, I will change you into four different colors." He also gave them two tablets of knowledge and a warning: do not cast them upon the ground, for if you do, humans and even the earth itself will have a difficult time.

The Great Spirit also gave the new nations a responsibility — a guardianship. To the Red nation of the east, he gave the Native tribes and Nations guardianship over the earth. The Native people bore the responsibility of familiarizing themselves with the plants of the earth. Particularly the ones for food and the ones for medicine and healing. When your brothers and sisters come back together, you will understand and prosper. *Much of the starchy and carbohydrate-rich grains were discovered, cultivated, and mass produced by these red people. Foodstuffs which would sustain humans the world over.*

The peoples of the south (Asia) received guardianship of the wind from The Great Spirit. They were charged with learning about the sky and breathing. *Could this be why the Moors were so interested in astronomy? So much so that even today, many of the stars in our constellations have Arabic names. For instance, in the Orion the Hunter constellation, the star Rigel is Arabic for "the left foot of The Great One." The Chinese would master the ability to explode gunpowder in the sky, as fireworks, to signal to the Great Spirit their conquest of the wind and sky.*

In the west, which is as black as the night itself, the black race was entrusted with guardianship of the chief element of water. It is no secret the importance water plays in human life and how it *surrounds the continent of Africa and how its mightiest civilization grew from the banks of the Nile River. As our Cherokee cousins and the Cherokee Freedmen say: "Ama nvgida" or "Water is life."*

In the north, where its people are as white as the snow-covered forests of Europe, these people were tied to the guardianship of fire. The element of fire was not only for geographic survival but would come to define the white nation. The light bulb is a contained fire, much like the internal combustible engine, and the locomotive moves and consumes like an approaching prairie fire. Therefore, the people of the north are most responsible for traversing the globe and ultimately bringing the separated people back together — *whether by colonization, cooperation (alliances/ economic endeavors), invasion/ warfare, or the information superhighway.*

Throughout time, these four groups of people have had chances to come together in a sacred circle to make peace and to promote mutual prosperity amongst nations. The prophecies were told to the people so they could remember the sacredness of all things and bring about peace on earth. If not, then The Great Spirit would grab the earth with His hand and shake it. After many signs would come to pass (east-west highways, cars, the airplane, etc.), the brothers and sisters of the four directions would spurn peace and The Great Spirit would cause the First Great Shaking of the earth. This would be the Great War, or what is now called World War I.

After the First Great Shaking, the governments of the world would come together in a sacred circle and talk about peace. This was the attempt at a lasting League of Nations; but no red nations were invited. Inevitably, more signs would come to pass (telephone wires, genocide, atomic weapons) and the hearts of man would grow cold and cunning yet again. The rise of fascism in the nations of the northern peoples, and imperialism in the rising sun nation in the west would give rise to the events of WWII, or the Second Great Shaking of the earth. Perhaps the most worrisome sign within the second Great Shaking is the story of the *gourd of ashes*. If one were to flip a gourd upside-down, you would see the familiar shape of a mushroom cloud. The gourd of ashes foretold the atomic devastation that the citizens of Hiroshima and Nagasaki would suffer. Burnt alive like so many blades of grass, consumed by a voracious and all-consuming brushfire.

To make a second attempt at bringing the people of the four directions together, they would establish the United Nations at the end of WWII. The Hopi prophecies also foretold the formation of the United Nations when it declared that they would "build a house of mica" to host the council fire. Mica is a flaky and brittle mineral which is noted for its brilliant shine, much like the glass facade of the UN building in New York City.

Another sign between the Second and Third Great Shaking of the earth would be when the Eagle flies so high that it lands on the moon. In 1969, the "Eagle has landed" was the radio transmission heard around the world when the United States put a man on the moon. Also, the Hopi speak of a time when mankind will put a house in the sky and people will live there for long periods of time. This represents the International Space Station (ISS). As for the United Nations, they foretold that this political body would not eradicate war, but would cause much confusion, which would spawn many wars, consuming more of humanity with an increase of destructive violence. *(See Africa, Ukraine, the Middle East, etc.)*

The Third Great Shaking sees the ones who dropped the gourd of ashes in WWII being consumed by the same weapon. How do we know that the Third Shaking is upon us? In the 1950s and 1960s, the Hopi foretold a time when men would become women. They would say to the Great Spirit, "I am not a man, and I am going to change myself to be a woman and they will even *nurse* children!" *Just think how absurd this must have sounded in the 1950s. Fast forward to the current day, where the LGBTQ+ movement is inescapable. A modern contagion of the highest degree of mental illness and identity instability.* Where women say, "I know more than the Great Spirit and I want to be a man" and she would become a man. *This is the epitome of the anti-Great Spirit; the Antichrist ushered into prominence by the "oppressed" cult of the transsexuals.* This is not the laws of nature, nor the wishes of the Great Spirit and He is set to grab the earth yet again — only this time He will shake it with both hands!

The symbol known as the swastika is present on the Hopi Prophecy Rock in Arizona. The swastika is a four-armed cross, representing the four directions, the four winds, the four peoples; only this cross has each of its four arms bent at 90-degree angles. *This* — THIS! — *is the 90-degree tilt of our world that men like Velikovsky, Einstein, and Chan Thomas warned us about. The Great Spirit watches as the world He created rolls over and 99% of His creation learns a hard lesson in obedience.* An event called the "Great Purification" will set things right for humanity's few survivors and usher in the fifth world. The Great Spirit purified the earth by ending the first world with fire, and the second world with ice. The third world was ended in Noah's Great Flood and the fourth will be ended by all manner of destruction: wind, fire, flood, and warfare. Will we learn to keep the earth and all of its living things sacred during the time of the fifth world? To be determined...

Chapter 5

The Ancient Ones and Men of Renown

*"In a single day and night of misfortune all your warlike men
in a body sank into the earth, and the island of Atlantis in like
manner disappeared in the depths of the sea."*

– Plato, *Timaeus*

As a Native American and a Christian, I have often questioned why we in the modern world discount or denounce the knowledge, stories, and legends of ancient civilizations. It would seem antithetical to build our modern world upon the earliest foundations of our own understanding of the world, only to now outright dismiss this knowledge as myth or fantastical tales by simple people. The statement "What could these primitive sorcerers possibly know about our modern lives?" comes to mind when thinking about this very topic.

I would argue that modernity turns its collective backs on ancient knowledge and warnings at its own peril. Take this offering from the Book of Enoch when juxtaposed next to the story you just read. From Chapter 65:1-3:

> 1) "And, in those days, Noah saw the Earth had tilted and that its destruction was near. 2) And he set off from there, and went to the ends of the Earth, and cried out to his great-grandfather Enoch; and Noah said three times in a bitter voice: "Hear me, hear me, hear me!" 3) And he said to him: "Tell me, what is it that is being done on the Earth, that the Earth is so afflicted, and shaken, lest I be destroyed with it!"
>
> — Enoch 65:1-3

If read with a keen eye, you see and hear more than just the words of the Old Testament. You also hear the words of the Hopi prophecy and Dr. Immanuel Velikovsky! Or take these verses, also from Enoch, and recall the reading of the Hopi prophecy:

> "And a command has gone out from the Lord, against those who dwell upon the dry ground, that this must be their end. For they have learnt all the secrets of the Angels, and all the wrongdoings of the satans, and all their secret power, and all the power of those who practice magic arts, and the power of enchantments, and the power of those who cast molten images for all the Earth."
>
> — Enoch 65:6

The Hopi said, "Once we are immersed into the cycle of the human being, *the highest and greatest powers that we have will be released to us.*" However, the people of the earth faced God's wrath:

> "And He [God] said to me: 'Because of their iniquity, their judgement has been completed, and they will no longer be counted before Me; because of the sorceries they have searched out, and learnt, the Earth and those who dwell upon it will be destroyed."
>
> — Enoch 65:10

We see a similar warning from Daniel, which also mirrors the Hopi allusion to *the highest and greatest powers.* Perhaps we should look back to Adam and Eve in the garden of Eden, in which God forbade them from eating from "the tree of knowledge of good and evil." Since the beginning of time, humanity has been in hot pursuit of gaining more knowledge. In the digital age, all the knowledge of the cosmos seems to stretch to infinity.

> "But thou, O Daniel, shut up the words, and seal the book, even to the time of the end: many shall run to and fro, and knowledge shall be increased."
>
> — Daniel 12:4

The Book of Joshua captures what conditions will be like when the solar micro nova unlocks the earth's crust:

> "And the sun stood still, and the moon stayed, until the people had avenged themselves upon their enemies. Is not this written in the book of Jasher? So the sun stood still in the midst of heaven, and hasted not to go down about a whole day."
>
> — Joshua 10:13

In the Old Testament book of Isaiah, chapter 24 paints a vivid warning from the Almighty:

> 1) Behold, the Lord maketh the earth empty, and maketh it waste, and turneth it upside down, and scattereth abroad the inhabitants thereof. 2) And it shall be, as with the people, so with the priest; as with the servant, so with his master; as with the maid, so with her mistress; as with the buyer, so with the seller; as with the lender, so with the borrower; as with the taker of usury, so with the giver of usury to him. 3) The land shall be utterly emptied, and utterly spoiled: for the Lord hath spoken this word. 4) The earth mourneth and fadeth away, the world languisheth and fadeth away, the haughty people of the earth do languish. 5) The earth also is defiled under the inhabitants thereof; because they have transgressed the laws, changed the ordinance, broken the everlasting covenant. 6) Therefore hath the curse devoured the earth, and they that dwell therein are desolate: therefore the inhabitants of the earth are burned, and few men left. 7) The new wine mourneth, the vine languisheth, all the merryhearted do sigh. 8) The mirth of tabrets ceaseth, the noise of them that rejoice endeth, the joy of the harp ceaseth. 9) They shall not drink wine with a song; strong drink shall be bitter to them that drink it. 10) The city of confusion is broken down: every house is shut up, that no man may come in. 11) There is a crying for wine in the streets; all joy is darkened, the mirth of the land is gone.

12) In the city is left desolation, and the gate is smitten with
destruction. 13) When thus it shall be in the midst of the land
among the people, there shall be as the shaking of an olive tree,
and as the gleaning grapes when the vintage is done. 14) They
shall lift up their voice, they shall sing for the majesty of the
Lord, they shall cry aloud from the sea. 15) Wherefore glorify
ye the Lord in the fires, even the name of the Lord God of
Israel in the isles of the sea. 16) From the uttermost part of the
earth have we heard songs, even glory to the righteous. But I
said, My leanness, my leanness, woe unto me! the treacherous
dealers have dealt treacherously; yea, the treacherous dealers
have dealt very treacherously. 17) Fear, and the pit, and the
snare, are upon thee, O inhabitant of the earth. 18) And it shall
come to pass, that he who fleeth from the noise of the fear shall
fall into the pit; and he that cometh up out of the midst of the
pit shall be taken in the snare: for the windows from on high
are open, and the foundations of the earth do shake. 19) The
earth is utterly broken down, the earth is clean dissolved, the
earth is moved exceedingly. 20) The earth shall reel to and fro
like a drunkard, and shall be removed like a cottage; and the
transgression thereof shall be heavy upon it; and it shall fall,
and not rise again. 21) And it shall come to pass in that day,
that the Lord shall punish the host of the high ones that are on
high, and the kings of the earth upon the earth.

— Isaiah 24:1-21

There are those within and without want for the Christian traditions
who might say, "those are old teachings. What of the New Testament and
not the angry God of the Old Testament?" After all, the New Testament
God is full of grace, love, and mercy. The warnings of signs to come do not
stop with the crucifixion of Jesus Christ. In Matthew 24:3, the disciples
ask Jesus, *"what shall be the sign of thy coming, and of the end of the world?"*
Jesus answers:

6) "And ye shall hear of wars and rumours of wars: see that ye be not troubled: for all these things must come to pass, but the end is not yet. 7) For nation shall rise against nation, and kingdom against kingdom: and there shall be famines, and pestilences, and earthquakes, in divers places. 8) All these are the beginning of sorrows. 9) Then shall they deliver you up to be afflicted, and shall kill you: and ye shall be hated of all nations for my name's sake."

– Matthew 24:6-9

Where to begin? We humans still have not figured out how to prevent wars amongst nations. In fact, the ongoing war in Ukraine may very well precipitate the next great famine of modern history. This is especially the case now that the highest and greatest powers of the uranium atom (NATO-supplied Depleted Uranium munitions, or DU) are being used against the invading Russian Army while simultaneously poisoning the Ukrainian environment. Contaminated groundwater will now supply this farmland, known as the "Breadbasket of Europe," with the required water to grow vast amounts of grain. For pestilence, one needs only look back to the COVID-19 pandemic of 2020 for validation (and that virus continues to mutate!). Earthquakes are indeed increasing in both their frequency and intensity. This will only get worse due to earth's magnetic shield continuing to weaken!

The warnings of the Book of Matthew continue with insight into the mental status of mankind prior to the End Times:

10) "And then shall many be offended, and shall betray one another, and shall hate one another. 11) And many false prophets shall rise, and shall deceive many. 12) And because iniquity shall abound, the love of many shall wax cold."

– Matthew 24:10-12

Does any of this sound familiar? The easily offended and enraged gave birth to cancel culture and doxing. Social media, mass media, and mis-/disinformation campaigns run amuck in our current news cycle. Lawlessness and an overall lack of morality plague men's hearts today!

> 15) "When ye therefore shall see the abomination of desolation, spoken of by Daniel the prophet, stand in the holy place, (whoso readeth, let him understand:) 16) Then let them which be in Judaea flee into the mountains: 17) Let him which is on the housetop not come down to take any thing out of his house: 18) Neither let him which is in the field return back to take his clothes. 19) And woe unto them that are with child, and to them that give suck in those days! 20) But pray ye that your flight be not in the winter, neither on the sabbath day: 21) For then shall be great tribulation, such as was not since the beginning of the world to this time, no, nor ever shall be. 22) And except those days should be shortened, there should no flesh be saved: but for the elect's sake those days shall be shortened."
>
> – Matthew 24:15-22

Earth fire, earthquakes, and tsunami flood waters will conquer the lands at low elevation once the solar micro nova unleashes its fury upon our terrestrial home. Persons stranded on rooftops bring back memories of the aftermath of Hurricane Katrina. Woe indeed to those survivors post-pole shift/ post-micro nova who find themselves rotated to one of the new poles, where icecaps will form almost immediately. As for the shortened days, this is already happening! In 2020, scientists reported that earth experienced 28 of the shortest days ever. The speeding up of the earth's rotation could be a harbinger of the crust unlocking and continuing its movement via the Dzhanibekov Effect, or intermediate axis theorem as it is often called.

Staying in Matthew chapter 24, verse 29 continues with:

> "Immediately after the tribulation of those days shall the sun be darkened, and the moon shall not give her light, and the

stars shall fall from heaven, and the powers of the heavens shall be shaken:"

– Matthew 24:29

This prose and imagery paint a vivid picture of the transition of our once yellow sun to the white sun, then red, then black in the moments prior to blasting its plasma shell out across the solar system.

Matthew continues to highlight the destruction awaiting us on the day our sun goes micro nova. I urge you to reread the Book of Genesis if any doubt lingers regarding whether we are presently living in the days of Noah!

> 37) But as the days of Noah were, so shall also the coming of the Son of man be. 38) For as in the days that were before the flood they were eating and drinking, marrying and giving in marriage, until the day that Noe entered into the ark, 39) And knew not until the flood came, and took them all away; so shall also the coming of the Son of man be."

– Matthew 24:37-39

I will leave you with one additional New Testament warning from the Book of Luke, chapter 21. Think back to the cosmic signs and health issues discussed in a previous chapter as you ponder these words:

> 25) "And there shall be signs in the sun, and in the moon, and in the stars; and upon the earth distress of nations, with perplexity; the sea and the waves roaring; 26) Men's hearts failing them for fear, and for looking after those things which are coming on the earth: for the powers of heaven shall be shaken."

– Luke 21:25-26

We have been warned, many times, by many people, and from every corner of the earth. Modernity, with its systems of globalism, humanism, and neo-liberalism, leave humanity with no viable options to prevent the storm on our horizon. I invite you to turn away from groups, to look not unto technology, which is doomed to failure by our own star, but to search your heart and what you have read on these pages. I have some great news for every single person reading these words! This world has a *saving grace* despite the calamity awaiting us. I beg you to repent and give your heart and soul to the one who created our universe. Romans 10:9 tells us:

> "If you declare with your mouth, "Jesus is Lord," and believe in your heart that God raised him from the dead, you will be saved."
>
> – Romans 10:9

People have asked me how I can reconcile being a professed Christian while also holding onto the traditions of my Native American lineage. My answer is quite simple. My 12th Great-Grandfather, upon being presented with a preponderance of evidence to the birth, life, teachings, fulfillment of prophecy, crucifixion, death, and resurrection of Jesus Christ, converted to Christianity and became the first Native American to be baptized into the Christian church. The day was August 13, 1587, and Chief Manteo of present-day coastal North Carolina was baptized into the Anglican (Protestant Christian) Church. On that day, Manteo was more than an ambassador, peacemaker, warrior, and chief; as a child of God and heir to the Heavenly Kingdom, he became so much more!

Join us. Jesus Christ, the Great Peacemaker of the Book of Revelation, is the bridge between two worlds: the *Living* and the *Dead*. God will certainly destroy the earth one day; maybe sooner than any of us would like. However, you need not share its fate. Jesus Christ has made a way — The Way! — for you to have everlasting life. Once you are His, no fire from Hell, nor rising flood waters shall rob you of His gift. Wado, Unetlanvhi. Wado ale gvgeyui, Tsisa! {from Cherokee: Thank you, Our Creator. Thank you and I love you, Jesus!} Aho. Amen.

Chapter 6

Blackout

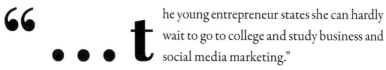

66 ... t he young entrepreneur states she can hardly wait to go to college and study business and social media marketing."

With a slight laugh and smile, head anchor Chuck Lawrence turns back to camera one before commenting, "we'll have to keep a lookout for this motivated four-year-old. When we come back from the break, former NASA scientist and space weather alarmist Dave Bennett will join us to talk about the upcoming solar maximum cycle for our sun."

"That's right, Chuck," nods on-air personality LaShonda Briggs, "what could this mean for global climate change and the 2032 hurricane season?" The desk producer signals for a commercial break and the familiar Bold City News 7 music plays as camera one slowly bleeds out for the television audience. LaShonda reviews notes from the production meeting earlier in the day while waiting for Dave Bennett to join them on set.

Chuck gives a thumbs-up in the affirmative to the control room after receiving instructions via his earpiece from the Bold City News 7 producer. He and LaShonda are making small talk when their guest of the hour walks up to the set and takes a seat to the left of the news anchors. The three of them exchange pleasantries with smiles before Chuck gets down to business. "Mr. Bennett, a friendly reminder that in the course of our on-air discussion, we must be cognizant and sensitive to any speech deemed non-compliant to the disinformation guidelines set forth by the IPCC."

Dave could not resist a slight chuckle at the mention of the United Nations' Intergovernmental Panel on Climate Change (IPCC). For that fact, he detested any and every governmental body that infringed upon the First Amendment or anything protected by the Constitution of the United States of America. The idea of censorship of scientific endeavor because it does not fit some globalist narrative was enough to make him foam at the mouth on his popular podcast Got Micro Nova? "No need to worry," Dave said with a wry grin. "I assure you I am well versed on the IPCC muzzle."

Sensing a bit of tension, LaShonda Briggs jumped into the fray with, "now boys; let's play nice!" Her warm smile and gentle, motherlike voice cooled things down just in time for their 10-second live telecast warning. LaShonda cleared her throat and Chuck straightened his Armani coat with a quick downward tug as the red light on camera one turned to a bright green color and the stage director pointed at Chuck.

"Now we pivot from today's headlines for a much-anticipated interview with space weather enthusiast, Mr. Dave Bennett. Most of you know of Dave's work on the social media sensation known as the Got Micro Nova? podcast, website, and national tour." Chuck turned his chair to the left and faced his guest before asking, "So, why space weather? What initially got you interested in the topic which many of our viewers might be hearing about for the first time?"

Dave sat up extra tall in his chair and answered, "I got my start in exploring space weather by asking intelligent questions and challenging friends of mine back home in North Carolina who are highly thought of professors, researchers, and scientists. After all, life on earth could not exist without our sun and I think most would agree it is directly responsible for our wonderful, life-giving climate that humanity enjoys."

"To be clear, Dave," LaShonda injects, "you are addressing the sun's activity regarding things like sunspots, solar flares, and solar storms, yes?"

"Yes. More importantly, I have brought attention to the relationship between solar storms, the cyclical existence of the solar micro nova, and the earth's weakening magnetic field. Put these things together and soon one realizes we are in big, big trouble."

Chuck pounces at the opportunity to reinforce the mainstream notion, and as of 2028, national and international law mandating communication of the Anchorage Accords. "A quick note to our audience," interjects the matter-of-fact anchorman, "we are intentionally going to avoid some of the more, shall we say — controversial opinions Mr. Bennett has defended over the past decade." The Anchorage Accords, ratified into law unequivocally codifies any media (television, print, social media, etc.) concerning all topics related to global climate change and robustly reinforces the imperative that our planet is warming. Not only is it warming, but it is doing so exclusively because of human causes vis-à-vis carbon dioxide, the production, refining, and consumption of hydrocarbons, and the production/farming and subsequent consumption of animal products. Ben always gets riled up at the focus on dreaded cow farts while ignoring the obtuse and ignorant hot air being expelled by worthless politicians! Ben was prepared to pull his punches, knowing the censorship Gestapo would fine him nearly to death for daring to question the political narrative.

"I will do my best to keep my money in my bank account and not surrender a single dime to IPCC bureaucrats, thanks," Dave bristles. "All jokes aside, our best educated guess is that the earth's magnetic field has weakened anywhere from 30 to 35% since the 1859 Carrington event, which melted telegraph wires. If that same event were to take place today, it would be catastrophic. I assure you I am not being flippant or bombastic in that opinion based on very real science."

LaShonda Briggs moves the conversation forward to a list of questions approved by her producer. "I think most of us are aware of the Carrington event. However, you have made a controversial claim that increasing temperatures seen around the world are not the real problem. That the future of our planet is cold."

"Well, maybe controversial to some," Dave says while choking back a laugh, "but if one looks objectively at the data, then the prospect of the Beaufort Gyre being released into the north Atlantic, the shutdown of the Atlantic Meridional Overturning Current, and the subsequent freezing of Europe is far more alarming than the alternative."

Without warning, the cameras abruptly switch to standby, leaving the co-anchors wondering what happened to their feed. "What's going on, Martin?" demands Chuck Lawrence from the news desk.

"Sorry, guys. The Pentagon commandeered all network live feeds for an update on the North Korea situation. We'll have to reschedule our guest. My apologies. Sit tight, you two."

Great, Dave thought to himself. They've got another thing coming if they think I'm dying to come back to Jacksonville. It will take an army to get me off of my North Carolina mountaintop!

*   *   *

The Smith family is enjoying the sun-splashed Saturday morning gathered around their backyard swimming pool. No one has any plans today other than getting a tan and taking a nap. Scott Smith is just happy he does not need to go into the office today to catch-up on work. His son attempts to swim laps, but he is flailing about so much that the swimming pool resembles a washing machine. "Chase! That's some mighty expensive water you are throwing all over the place!"

"Sorry, dad," Chase replied in between inhaling huge gasps of air.

"Honey, can you please teach him how to swim properly before he has an asthma attack, or worse?" prods his wife, Vanessa.

"Yes, dear."

Courtney chimes with typical big sister commentary. "Now you know why I never want to be anywhere near him when he's in the pool!" Her five years younger brother answered this bit of mild derision with a giant splash which covered Courtney head-to-toe. Courtney's screaming drowned Chase's laughter out, and the first fight of the day ensued. Now Scott was thinking maybe a couple hours of quiet office time wouldn't be such a bad thing after all.

Vanessa broke up the fight by scolding Chase and agreeing to help Courtney reapply her suntanning lotion, but not before a lecture about not getting too much sun. Vanessa restored calm and everyone could hear music playing from Vanessa's cell phone once more. Out of nowhere, the lyrics to everyone's favorite New Year's Eve song stopped short of announcing the command to "party like it's 1999."

"Your phone died, sweetie?" asked Jeff. "My charger should be inside on the bar if you want to grab it. Or you can just use mine." Jeff leaned over to retrieve his phone but stopped short of tossing it to his wife when he noticed his phone had shut down as well.

"You can just listen to whatever music you want to," replied Vanessa. "I'll charge my phone later."

"I know good and well my phone had a full charge, but my phone won't turn back on."

"I warned y'all," added Courtney, "our old network doesn't work half the time out here." By out here, she meant their new home on Sullivan's Island, South Carolina.

"Dad! The pool's not working anymore!" exclaimed Chase with visible disappointment. Sure enough, the waterfall feature from the hot tub had shut off and water was no longer spilling over down to the pool or being pumped through the pool's motor.

That's odd, Jeff thought to himself. "I see that, buddy. Hold on a second. I'll check the breaker box in the garage. Maybe we had a power surge." Jeff hopped up, exited the lanai door from the pool, and made his way to the keypad for the garage door. He entered the six-digit code and hit enter, but nothing happened. "Come on!" Jeff complained out loud to no one. "Three-one-one-two-zero-four. Enter," Jeff repeated out loud to ensure he was doing it right. Still nothing. Frustrated and confused, Jeff walked out to the front of the house to see if the unwanted power outage also afflicted everyone else along Middle Street.

Determining if the lights were functioning was challenging, as the sun had already risen. However, Jeff could not hear any lawnmowers or leaf blowers which were almost guaranteed to fill the air on any given

Saturday morning. What he heard was a strange crashing sound, followed by the sound of cars crashing together. This all too familiar sound was from working in downtown Charleston and being unfortunate enough to get caught in a customary evening downpour while attempting to leave work for the day. Apparently, Charlestonians had never received the notice that hydroplaning happens when it rains.

Jeff slowly jogged to the end of the street to get a better view of Charleston harbor when he overheard some kids talking about a helicopter crashing into a private pier. That's when his attention snapped back to reality as he noticed a commercial airliner crashing into a crane in downtown Charleston! Jeff took off in a dead sprint for his home and family.

Jeff startled Vanessa and Courtney when he burst back into the lanai, completely out of breath. "My God! What is the matter?" his wife begged. Before he could answer, something prompted the family to look straight up when a shadow had all but blocked out the surrounding sunshine. Jeff could tell that the shadow was from a Charleston Air Force Base C-17 cargo plane.

Vanessa ran over to her husband's side once the behemoth plane had passed. Scott's eyes met hers and the only words that came to his mind to share were, "It's happened."

"What happened?"

Scott was searching for his thoughts and ignored Vanessa's question. He finally asked his own question out loud and seemingly to himself, "Why didn't they warn us?"

Chase started crying and Vanessa grabbed Jeff's chin and forced his gaze up to lock eyes with her. "What's happening, Scott?"

"It's like Carrington all over again," he replied to his now visibly worried wife. After a brief pause, he added, "Or much, much worse."

TO BE CONTINUED...

About The Author

C. Elmon Meade is an award-winning Sci-Fi, Christian Thriller, and Dystopian Fiction author (Feed My Reads 2022 Sci-Fi Novel of the Year for *The Demagogue Wars*). With 15 years of combined military experience - eight in the U.S. Army and seven in the USAF and the South Carolina Air National Guard - C. Elmon Meade served in Korea, Saudi Arabia, and Kuwait. He currently works in finance as a Lean Six Sigma Master Black Belt certified process engineer. He holds a BA in geography with a cognate in criminal justice from the University of South Carolina. Born in North Carolina, C. Elmon is a member of the Coharie Tribe with ancestors of Cherokee, Tuscarora, Lumbee, and Powhatan descent. He currently lives in Jacksonville, Florida and enjoys genealogy and visiting Florida beaches. He is also a member of Christ's Church in Jacksonville.

Credits

1. Front cover image (photo credit): NASA Scientific Visualization Studio. Solar Dynamics Observatory image from https://svs.gsfc.nasa.gov/11473/

2. Back cover image (photo credit): Hopi image via Wikimedia Commons. (Public Domain) https://commons.wikimedia.org/wiki/File:Petroglyph_Point_at_Mesa_Verde_National_Park_by_RO.JPG#filelinks (Public domain)

3. Back cover image (photo credit): Dead Sea scrolls image. Public domain. https://en.wikipedia.org/wiki/4Q246 (Public domain)

4. Gentile, AJ, Gentile, Gino, Gentile, Jennifer. "CIA Classified Book about the Pole Shift, Mass Extinctions and The True Adam & Eve Story" via YouTube (Premiered Jan 12, 2023). The Why Files: Operation Podcast. https://www.youtube.com/watch?v=4n3fkTq_p0o&t=894s Video length = 27:08.

5. Davidson, Ben. "THE NEXT DISASTER | Part 1 - Ice, Fire, Magnetism" via YouTube (Dec 25, 2020). Suspicious 0bservers. https://www.youtube.com/watch?v=V2decDcE-Jqo&list=PLHSoxioQtwZcVcFC85TxEEiirgfXwhfsw&index=1 Video length = 6:43.

6. Davidson, Ben. "Earth Catastrophe Cycle | 2019 Original Series" via YouTube (Last updated on Feb 24, 2020). Suspicious 0bservers. 27 videos viewable at:

https://www.youtube.com/
playlist?list=PLHSoxioQtwZcVLEJjpywllxdsEfJjoOQ3

7. Smith, Joel. "Lee Brown - Native American Prophecies 1 & 2"
   via YouTube (Mar 4, 2015). YouTube channel = @joel smith.
   https://www.youtube.com/watch?v=u3mzk__aa-o&t=898s
   Video length = 1:11:56.